Weekly Reader Children's Book Club presents

How Many Dragons Are Behind the Door?

written and illustrated
by Virginia Kahl

CHARLES SCRIBNER'S SONS · NEW YORK

Printed in the United States of America/1 3 5 7 9 11 13 15 17 19 RD/C 20 18 16 14 12 10 8 6 4 2
Library of Congress Catalog Card Number 76-57961/ISBN 0-684-14906-0

Weekly Reader Children's Book Club Edition

Long ago, in a castle, far, far away,
A Duke and a Duchess were living, and they
Had a family of daughters whom they loved dearly.

One day they called them and counted out clearly.
The Duchess said, pointing, "One, two, three."
"That's all," said the Duke, "that I can see.
Oh, here is another girl, two, three, four."
"I'm sure," said the Duchess, "that we had more."

"Ah, here's number six, and there's number seven,
And eight, nine, and ten—and there is eleven.
Do you see any more? We need only two
To finish our task; let's name them all, too:

There's Madeleine, Gwendolyn, Jane, and Clothilde,
Caroline, Genevieve, Maude, and Mathilde,
Willibald, Guinevere, Joan, and Brunhilde,
And here is our youngest, our little Gunhilde."

She sighed with relief and said,
     "Girls, if you're good,
You can all take a walk
     to the edge of the wood.
But be sure to be home before the sun's set,
And don't pick up, please,
               an additional pet.
For we've rabbits and kittens,
               canaries and puppies,
Turtles and snakes and a bowl full
               of guppies,
Chickens and ducklings and lambkins
               and goats,
Ponies and piglets and hedgehogs and stoats."

So off ran the girls, down the path
       to the wood,
After telling the Duchess that they'd all be good.
One daughter, two daughters, three daughters, four,
Skipped down the steps and escaped through the door.
Five girls, six girls, seven girls, eight,
Marched in a line through the garden gate.
Hand in hand came nine and ten;
Eleven and twelve came after. Then
Came the thirteenth child, the only one
With no companion. That was no fun.

While most of the girls played
      among the flowers,
Gunhilde went off through the forest bowers.
She wandered slowly, and felt downhearted;
Then she saw that the bushy leaves
      had parted.
She heard a snort; then she saw
      some fire;
She looked on the ground;
      Then she looked higher.
And she looked all around
      down that forest track,
She saw a good-natured dragon
      staring back!

She turned and ran, with a shout of laughter,

And that amiable dragon galumphed on after.

After a time the other girls missed her.
"Where, oh where, is our littlest sister?
"Gunhilde! Gunhilde!
    Come back! Come back!"
Then they started to trace her
    down that forest track.

One called...

two called...

three called...

four.

Together they made the forest roar.

Then everyone called,
  "Gunhilde, dear.
It's time to go home.
  Come here!
  Come here!"

Then they spied, coming down that forest track,
A dragon, with Gunhilde seated on her back.
A fat, sleepy dragon, of enormous height.
"Are you certain," asked the girls,
        "that she won't bite?"

But they found that dragon so polite and kind
That the girls couldn't bear
            to make her stay behind.
"Do you think she's lost?
        Does she need a home?"
"It isn't right that she's been left
        to roam."
"And what will she do if it rains tonight?
We had better make sure that
        she'll be all right."

As all of her sisters crowded up beside her,
Gunhilde said, "Girls, maybe we should hide her?"

So they pushed her
through the entrance
of the highest tower,
Which was quite a change
from her leafy
bower.

And never a word did they
dare to speak
About the beast that they'd
brought home that week.

Each day the girls would
bring her buns for lunch,
And milk to drink,
and sweets to
munch.

She remained there, hidden, in that cozy place
While she grew fatter and ran out of space.

One night the Duchess found she couldn't rest;
So she put on her bonnet and then got dressed.
She thought she heard a groan,
    and she thought she saw a spark
Coming out of the tower that looked over the park.

"There's a fire!" she cried
        and ran off in a flurry.
She awoke all the others and said,
        "You'd better hurry!"

Then she climbed to the tower
    On that moonlit night
And ran to the upper room.
    What a fright!

She saw smoke and fire;
    She heard grunts and groans.

There stood a dragon with enormous bones!

When the Duke came running at her frantic call,

He exclaimed, "This beast may devour us all.

For I'm sure she has eaten well all of her life.

So—here go my daughters! Here goes my wife."

But he was mistaken; he spoke without thinking.

For the beast looked kind as she sat there blinking.

Then he asked, "Just how did a beast so fat

Find its way to our tower? Can you tell me that?

How did it get here? Who brought it home?

A dragon should be out where it can roam."

So the girls said, "Father, we disobeyed.

For *we* brought her home from her forest glade."

The Duke cried, "Hurry, now, get her out!"

When Gunhilde objected, he said,

  "Child, don't pout.

She'll be happier when she's outside and free.

Then you all can play with her merrily."

But they found that was easier said than done.
When they talked of putting her out to run,
It sounded so simple, without a doubt.
But that beast was so fat
       That she couldn't get out!

They pushed and they tugged;
   they pulled hard as they could;
For they hoped she'd return to that
       leafy wood.
But they couldn't budge her;
      and what is more,
They knew they'd never get her
      through the tower door.

"Well," said the Duchess,
          "we'll never, never
Remove her. She'll stay, I'm afraid,
              forever and ever."
She turned to Gunhilde.
"You thought you were kind.
But see what can happen
          if you girls don't mind."

They called out the army
     to ram down the tower.
But they had no success, though they worked for
     an hour.

They tried to entice the beast;
     Then they tried to use force.
They pushed with a battering ram;
     They pulled with a horse.

Each pushed alone;
          then they all pushed together.
They wanted her out in such lovely weather.
     But snug and serene the dragon sat;
          She didn't seem to worry
               that she was fat.

     The Duchess cried out,
          "Oh, alas and alack!
          We'll never see her
               amble down that
                    forest track!"

So she stayed in the tower,
growing fatter still,
Munching cakes and buns
and sweets until

The girls went to visit her
one early morn...

And saw that a little
dragon had been born!

A baby dragon!

Then they saw two!

When they looked around,
they saw quite a few!

"One dragon, two dragons,
three dragons, four!

Look, there's another one
behind the door.

Two, three, four, five—there's another!

Look behind the arras;
    You may find his brother."

Six dragons, seven dragons,
        eight came running.
"Mother, may we keep them?" cried the girls.
        "They're cunning."

Nine, ten, eleven, twelve.
        That was the end.
There were twelve little dragons

And the girls'
dragon friend!

The mother was thin after giving birth
To about the largest dragon family on the earth.
They found that the mother could be squeezed through the door.
"Get her out!" cried the Duchess, "before there are more!
But I'm glad," she acknowledged,
 "that you each have a friend.
And I'm even more happy that this visit will end."

"Girls, each pick a baby now
    and carefully take it
Out to the forest.
    I expect you can make it."

So— one girl, two girls, three girls, four,
Carried their dragons through the tower door.
Then five girls, six girls, seven girls, eight,
Ran with the babies
    through the garden gate.

Then nine, ten, eleven, and twelve little maids
Bore dragon babies to the forest glades.
And walking behind them,
     sedate and staid,
Was the dragon mother, with the
     smallest maid.

Twelve little dragons
were returned that day
To the leafy wood
where they could romp
and play.

And last of all,
at the very end,
Came Gunhilde,
with the mother,
her favorite friend.